A Dare for a Hare

For Molly, Amy, Lola and Nell. Be brave x – C F

For Orla Grace and her Nana, Christine Alicia.
(No better big sister, not anywhere.) – L M

ORCHARD BOOKS
First published in Great Britain in 2019 by The Watts Publishing Group
First published in paperback in 2020

1 3 5 7 9 10 8 6 4 2

Text © Charlie Farley, 2019 • Illustrations © Layn Marlow, 2019

The moral rights of the author and illustrator have been asserted.
All rights reserved. A CIP catalogue record for this book is
available from the British Library.

HB ISBN 978 1 40834 652 5 • PB ISBN 978 1 40834 653 2

Printed and bound in China

MIX
Paper from
responsible sources
FSC
www.fsc.org
FSC® C104740

Orchard Books
An imprint of Hachette Children's Group
Part of The Watts Publishing Group Limited
Carmelite House, 50 Victoria Embankment
London, EC4Y 0DZ

An Hachette UK Company
www.hachette.co.uk
www.hachettechildrens.co.uk

A Dare for a Hare

Charlie Farley   Layn Marlow

ORCHARD

Sunrise in the fields as spring fills the air,
Lighting a hollow, home of the hare,
Where two brothers yawn as the sun warms their fur,
Stretching long legs, beginning to stir.

First Harvey, the youngest, who just loves to play,
To leap and to lollop through each boisterous day.

Then big brother Buster who'd rather just nap,
And is meant to keep Harvey from any mishap.

'Oh, Harvey,' sighs Buster, 'stop rushing around.
I'm having a snooze, so don't make a sound.'

'But I'm Harvey the Hare, **AS BRAVE AS A BEAR!**
Oh, come and play, Buster. *Pleeease* give me a dare.'

'Okay,' Buster says,
'If I give you a dare,
Will you let me sleep
and keep out of my hair?'

'Yes! I'm Harvey, so there!
AS BRAVE AS A BEAR!
Nothing can scare me.
I'm the world's bravest hare!'

'I dare you to snatch a peach from the farm,
Keep clear of the cat, whose claws do such harm.
Climb up Bear Ridge, cross the bridge on Creekmoor,
And you'll be the bravest of hares evermore.'

But as Harvey speeds off to dare number one,
Buster thinks, 'Oh no! What have I done?
I'll follow him closely, but keep out of sight,
Just to make sure that my brother's all right.'

Harvey bounds onwards
with no time to stop,
To the farm with a jump
and a skip and a hop.
Where he sees the farm cat,
a fiery fat beast,
Known to enjoy a hare as a feast . . .

'I'm Harvey, so there!
AS BRAVE AS A BEAR!
Cats don't scare me. I'm the
world's bravest hare!'

And Harvey slinks slyly
through stacked apple kegs,
Past strawberries, chicken
coop, hens laying eggs.

Then triumphantly back,
a peach in his jaws . . .

. . . when fierce
Cat pounces,
bristling with
claws.

But Buster clamps down
on Cat's twisting tail,
Who stops in his tracks with
a **YOWL** and a **WAIL**…

While Harvey runs on,
not the faintest idea,
That Buster is keeping
his path safe and clear.

So Harvey heads up,
on to Bear Ridge,
Over Creekmoor to
the rickety bridge.

'I'm Harvey the Hare,

AS BRAVE AS A BEAR.

No, I'm braver! No bear could
give **ME** a scare!'

Then Harvey stops still.

His heart skips a beat.

There's a thing in his path
he did **NOT** plan to meet.

Scary and snarly,
Sharp claws on each paw,
Towering tall
With a very loud . . .

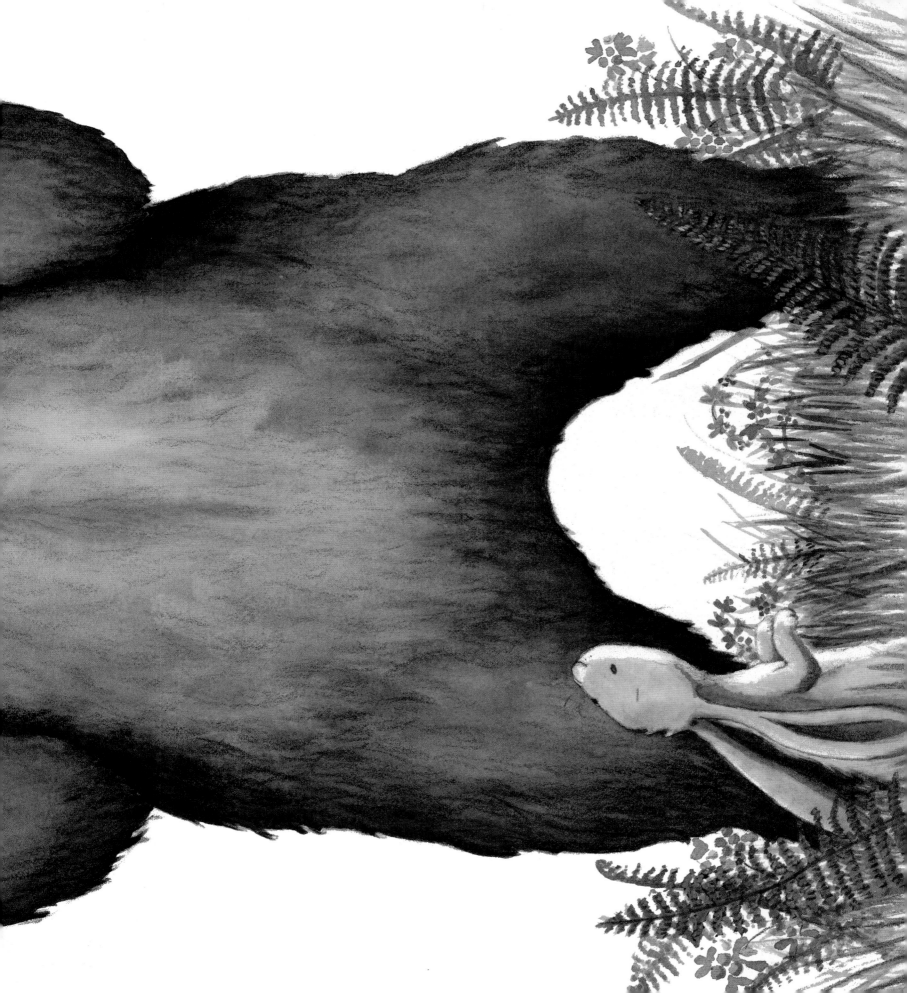

But Harvey is truly determined to win.

'I won't lose this dare!' So he sticks out his chin.

He musters his courage and closes his eyes,

And races past Bear, even though it's unwise.

Buster's dumbfounded as
Bear turns to chase,
Frozen in fear at their
hair-raising race.
A quick shake of his tail
gives Buster a jolt,
'I have to help Harvey,
this is all my fault.'

So as Harvey runs to the
bridge on the creek,
Big Bear on his tail, small legs
growing weak,

Buster bites down on the
bridge's worn rope,

The bridge starts to wobble . . .

a glimmer of hope!

And as Harvey jumps off
to land on the ground,
Ears over eyes, as he
daren't look around.
He hears Bear **HOWL**,
then an almighty . . .

SPLASH!

Big Bear in the river,
bridge toppling . . .

CRAsH!

Buster rushes to Harvey and gives him a hug,
'Come here, little brother, give my ears a tug!'

Harvey looks up, pulls his brother near,
And whispers, 'I win!' in Buster's big ear.
'I got a peach, beat the cat, crossed Creekmoor.'
'You win,' Buster smiles. 'You're the bravest for sure.'

'But, Buster,' says Harvey, 'I met a real bear,
So grumpy and grizzly, he gave me a scare.'

Buster looks at his brother, so small and so frail,
Curled up so tired with his trembling tail . . .

'No more dares, I'll never
leave your side again.'
'That suits me,' Harvey smiles,
'Let's doze on the plain.'

And slowly the brother
hares amble back home,
Whiskers just touching,
brave hearts fully grown.

As shadows get longer, the sun slips away,
Light turns to silver as night takes the day,
And two scruffy hares make one soft brown ball,
Adventures to dream as sleep starts to fall.

And half-asleep Harvey nuzzles his brother's ear.
'I know when you're with me I've nothing to fear . . .
You're Buster the Hare, **AS BRAVE AS A BEAR**,
No better big brother, not anywhere.'